BEAVER'S CRAZY SLEEPOVER

SEONG-MIN YOO

BEAVER'S CRAZY SLEEPOVER
SEONG-MIN YOO

Tumbleweed Books
Tumble through the pages of our books

Beaver's Crazy Sleepover / Seong min Yoo

ISBN 978-1-928094-51-7
EISBN 978-1-928094-52-4

The artwork in this book was rendered in watercolour, the text in Kristen ITC. Artwork and story by Seong min Yoo, Edit and layout by Douglas Owen

10 9 8 7 6 5 4 3 2 1

For Kum hwa and Bettie

Tonight is the special night Beaver has been waiting for all week.

As soon as she gets out of bed, she looks for a small backpack that mommy prepared last night,

and she carries it everywhere in the house
all day long, even when she takes a nap,

until she is ready to go, for a sleepover at Grandma's house, where the bubble bath is one of the most exciting moments of all.

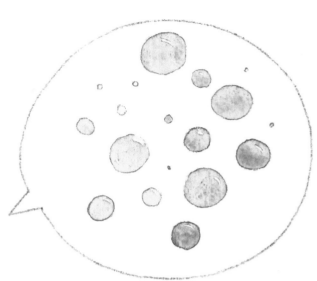

As she arrives at her house, she yells,
"I want bubble bath!"

"Before you do that, a little bit of stretching wouldn't hurt," Grandma says.

She holds up Beaver and
spins her around and
flips her over.

Beaver swings on Grandma's arms back and forth, and rides on her legs up and down.

"Ok, now."
Grandma winks at Beaver. Beaver smiles back at her.

Off they rush to
the kitchen.

"You know what? You need sweets to make a big splash," Grandma mumbles
with a big mouthful of cookies.

"Okay, Grandma," Beaver says
with a small
mouthful of cookies.

They both run to
the bedroom upstairs,

and Beaver slides off all her clothes just like that.

Off she goes into the bathtub and she jumps. "Yee-Haw!"

"Now here comes strong bubbles,"
Grandma shouts.

"Now here comes strong bubbles,"
Grandma shouts.

She gurgles under the water,

Grandma tickles Beaver's toes,
she wiggles her toes.

She gurgles under the water,

then she blows the bubbles all the way
to the top of her head.
"Ahhh! there's a bubble monster!"
Beaver cries.

"No, it's you, you're just all covered in the bubbles that you blew." Grandma cleans them from Beaver's eyes.

Grandma scrubs her feet.
Grandma scrubs her toes.
She hums. Beaver giggles.

"Here comes strong bubbles,"
they both exclaim with joy.

Beaver touches the bubbles
and they pop between her fingers,
more fingers and more toes
bring even greater pops,

and they mount all the way
to the top of Grandma's head.
This time she is all covered in bubbles

Grandma jumps and turns
and shakes them off
just like Beaver did.

"Now it's time to ...
bubble dance!" she shouts.

Here comes Grandma's silly moves.
One step,
two steps,
three steps,
cha cha cha!

Four bubbles,
five bubbles,
six bubbles,
pop, pop, pop!

Seven spins,
eight spins,
nine spins,
whee, whee ... whoa!
Grandma feels dizzy now.

"Grandma, faster, faster!"
Beaver claps and stomps.

So Grandma spins ten times faster.

Now her eyes are getting red,
her hair is all tangled,
and her clothes all soaked.

Grandma says to
Beaver, "Now, it's time
to relax and go to bed"

No !!!

On the way to the bedroom,
something caught her eyes.

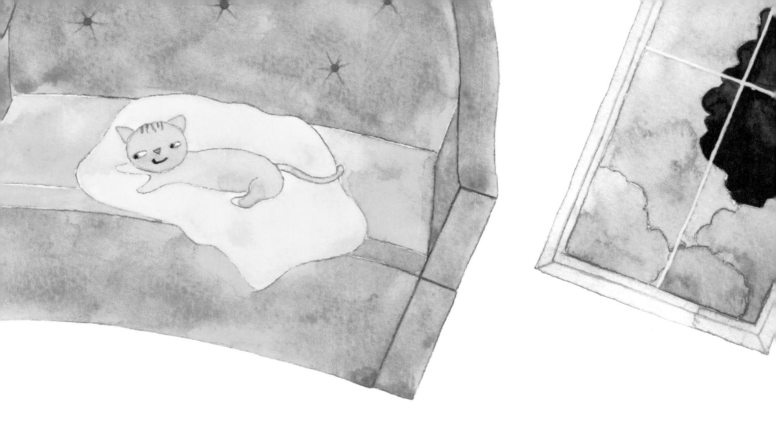

She jumped to it, munching the
chocolate caramel crunch
in front of the couch.

Here is totally exhausted Grandma,
with full-speed, non-stop Beaver
who's still giggling and jiggling.
"Now, it's time to rela..."

Before Grandma can say it,
she sees Beaver fall instantly
into a peaceful, sound sleep.

As Grandma touches her rosy cheeks,
she already misses the busy, dizzy,
bubbling joyous night they had together.